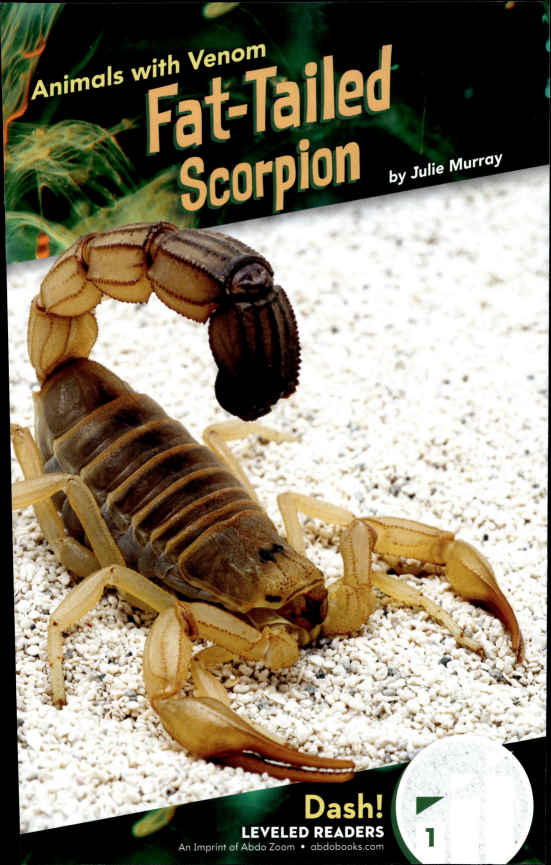

Animals with Venom
Fat-Tailed Scorpion
by Julie Murray

Dash!
LEVELED READERS
An Imprint of Abdo Zoom • abdobooks.com
1

Dash!
LEVELED READERS

Level 1 – Beginning
Short and simple sentences with familiar words or patterns for children who are beginning to understand how letters and sounds go together.

Level 2 – Emerging
Longer words and sentences with more complex language patterns for readers who are practicing common words and letter sounds.

Level 3 – Transitional
More developed language and vocabulary for readers who are becoming more independent.

THIS BOOK CONTAINS RECYCLED MATERIALS

abdobooks.com

Published by Abdo Zoom, a division of ABDO, PO Box 398166, Minneapolis, Minnesota 55439. Copyright © 2021 by Abdo Consulting Group, Inc. International copyrights reserved in all countries. No part of this book may be reproduced in any form without written permission from the publisher. Dash!™ is a trademark and logo of Abdo Zoom.

Printed in the United States of America, North Mankato, Minnesota.
052020
092020

Photo Credits: Alamy, iStock, Minden Pictures, Shutterstock, SuperStock
Production Contributors: Kenny Abdo, Jennie Forsberg, Grace Hansen, John Hansen
Design Contributors: Dorothy Toth, Neil Klinepier, Candice Keimig

Library of Congress Control Number: 2019956138

Publisher's Cataloging in Publication Data
Names: Murray, Julie, author.
Title: Fat-tailed scorpion / by Julie Murray.
Description: Minneapolis, Minnesota : Abdo Zoom, 2021 | Series: Animals with venom | Includes online resources and index.
Identifiers: ISBN 9781098221034 (lib. bdg.) | ISBN 9781644943984 (pbk.) | ISBN 9781098222017 (ebook) | ISBN 9781098222505 (Read-to-Me ebook)
Subjects: LCSH: Fat-tailed scorpions--Juvenile literature. | Scorpions--Juvenile literature. | Poisonous animals--Juvenile literature. | Scorpions--Venom--Juvenile literature. | Bites and stings--Juvenile literature.
Classification: DDC 591.69--dc23

Table of Contents

Fat-Tailed Scorpion 4

More Facts 22

Glossary 23

Index 24

Online Resources 24

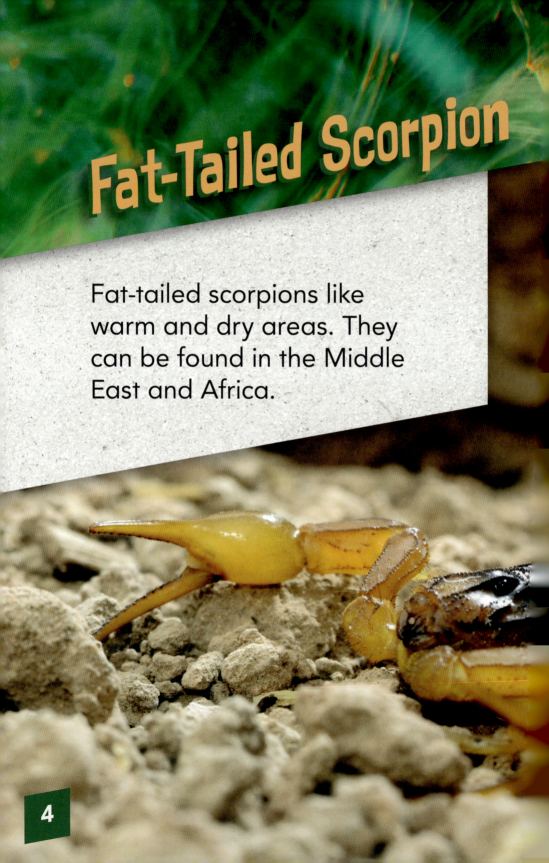

Fat-Tailed Scorpion

Fat-tailed scorpions like warm and dry areas. They can be found in the Middle East and Africa.

5

The fat-tailed scorpion hides under rocks or in holes during the day. It comes out at night.

Its name in Latin is *Androctonus*. This means "man killer" in English.

It is **aggressive**. It moves fast. Its **venom** can be deadly.

Most fat-tailed scorpions are black or brown in color. Some are reddish.

pincer

A fat-tailed scorpion has eight legs. It uses its **pincers** to fight or grab and crush **prey**.

It has a long, thick tail. The **stinger** is at the tip. This contains the **venom**.

stinger

The fat-tailed scorpion **injects** its **prey** with **venom**. Then the prey can no longer move.

Its **prey** includes lizards and insects. It also eats rodents.

More Facts

- A fat-tailed scorpion is about 3 to 4 inches (7.6-10 cm) long.

- There are more than 10 different kinds of fat-tailed scorpions found around Africa and the Middle East.

- A female fat-tailed scorpion can have 20 to 30 babies at a time.

Glossary

aggressive – unfriendly, forceful, and ready to fight.

inject – to put into with force through a stinger or fangs.

pincer – a claw of an animal.

prey – an animal that is hunted and eaten by another animal.

stinger – the sharp, pointed part of certain animals that sometimes carries poison. The stinger is used to wound others.

venom – the poison that certain animals make.

Index

Africa 4

color 12

food 15, 18, 21

habitat 4, 7

Latin 9

legs 15

Middle East 4

stinger 16

tail 16

venom 11, 16, 18

Online Resources

To learn more about the fat-tailed scorpion, please visit **abdobooklinks.com** or scan this QR code. These links are routinely monitored and updated to provide the most current information available.